Love

KU-675-918

BONNEY PRESS

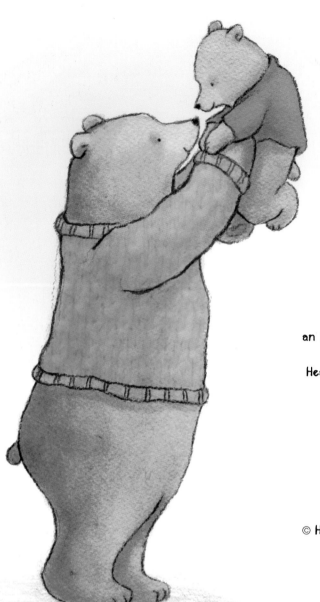

Laois County Library
Leabharlann Chontae Laoise
Acc. No. ...22/16197....
Class No. ....JPB........
Inv. No. .....16697.....

Published by Bonney Press,
an imprint of Hinkler Books Pty Ltd
45-55 Fairchild Street
Heatherton Victoria 3202 Australia
www.hinkler.com.au

BONNEY
PRESS

© Hinkler Books Pty Ltd 2014, 2016

Author: Helen O'Dare
Illustrator: Nicola O'Byrne

All rights reserved. No part of this publication may be reproduced, stored
in a retrieval system, or transmitted in any way or by any means, electronic,
mechanical, photocopying, recording or otherwise, without the prior written
permission of Hinkler Books Pty Ltd.

ISBN: 978 1 4889 2880 2

Printed and bound in Poland

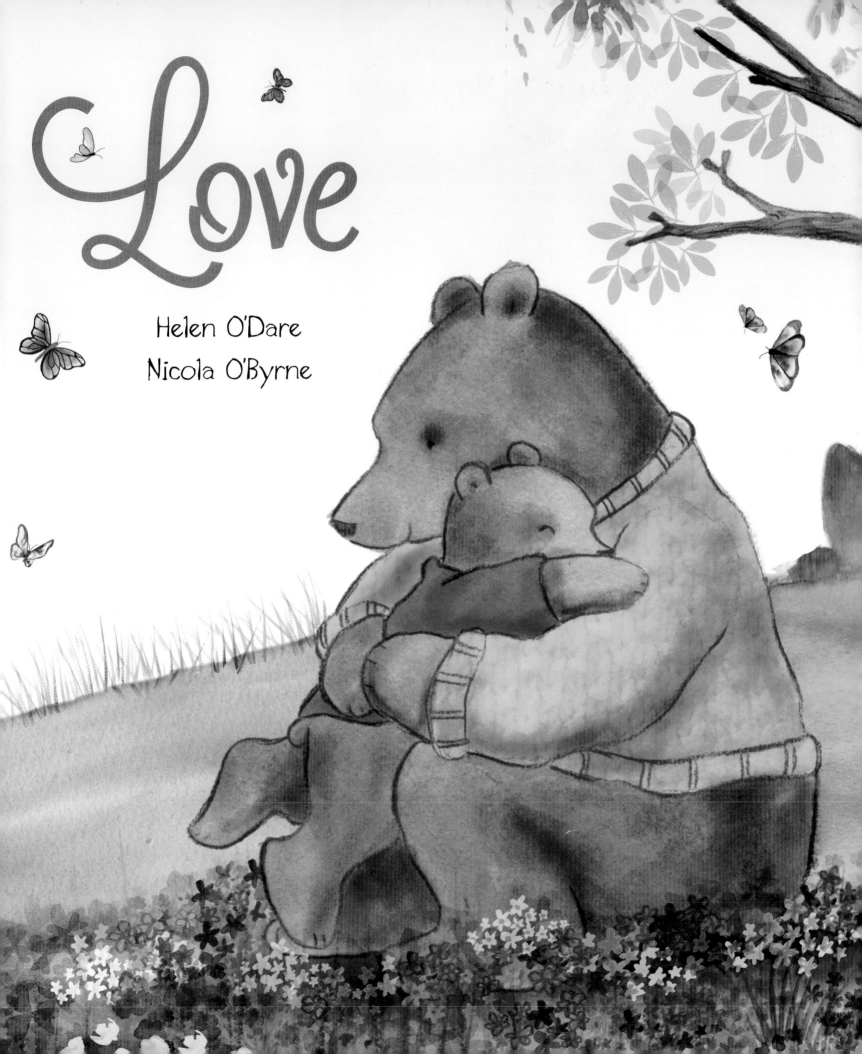

Love

Helen O'Dare

Nicola O'Byrne

This book is for all the special people in my life,
and especially for the most special of all, Reay and Bridie – HO'D

Love

can be **gigantic** like a **mountain**,
and **small** and **precious** like a **diamond**.

Love
stretches up, up, **tall** like a **tree**,
but secured by its **roots** so **deep**.

$\mathcal{L}$ove
has **wings** that help you **fly**
above the **clouds** in the **big blue sky**.

Love

is there in a **tickle** and a **giggle**
and an **enormous** belly-laugh **wiggle**!

Love

can be **loud** like a trumpet's **blares**
that sometimes **catch** you **unawares**!

Love

is a **book** and a **warm** milk mug,
and makes the **rainy** days all **snug**.

Love

can be **yummy,** like a **chocolate cake**
that we mixed and put in the **oven** to **bake.**

Love
can make you **sing** out **loud.**
You always make me feel so **proud!**

Love

can be **splashes** and **soap** and **bubbles**.
I will always **love** your **cuddles**!

Love

is **strong** and **true** like a **big bear hug**
that you give to a **sleepy** little **snuggle-bug**.

Love
is **big** and **wide**
and **ocean deep**.
It's even **there**
when you're **asleep**.

Love
is all of these, it's true.
And that's how much **I love YOU!**